I AM
THE BEST

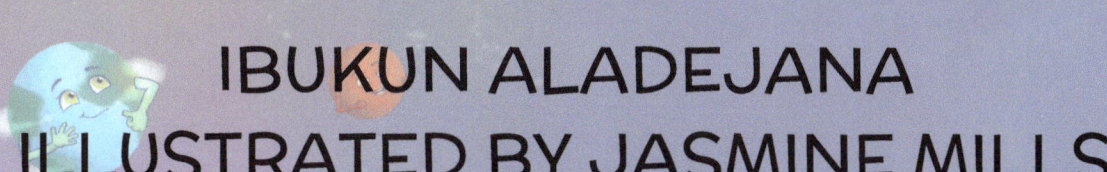

IBUKUN ALADEJANA
ILLUSTRATED BY JASMINE MILLS

To all the children in the world
you are the best.

INTRODUCTION

The God of the galaxy, The King of Kings and the Lord of Lords, created all things including the solar system.

The solar system is made up of the Sun, the eight official planets, at least 3 dwarf planets, more than 130 satellites, a large number of small bodies called comets and asteroids, and the interplanetary medium.

There are many more planetary satellites that are yet to be discovered but God the creator knows them all.

The inner solar system consists of the Sun, Mercury, Venus, Earth, and Mars. While Jupiter, Saturn, Uranus, and Neptune are the planets of the outer solar system.

"There is one glory of the sun, and another glory of the moon and another glory of the stars. Each differ from other in glory, but all glorify the creator,"

I am the largest object in the solar system. I contain more than 99.8% of the total mass of the Solar System. My magnetic field is very strong; I am a great instrument in God's hands, my creator commanded Joshua to tell me to stand still and not go down for some time so that God can save his children from the hands of some mean people and I stood still at his command.

When King Hezekiah was sick, my creator made me to go back 10 degrees to fulfill His promise to heal and deliver Israel from the hand of a mean king.

I shine my light on earth so that plants can use energy from me to make their food. I am the best.

I am the Sun

Hello, Mercury here!!! I am the best! I am the closest planet to the sun;

I am the smallest planet.

I am slightly smaller in diameter than the Earth's moon. My temperature is the most extreme in the solar system; I can go from 90 Kelvin to 700 Kelvin. This means I am very hot!

I have been visited by two space crafts, Mariner 10 and MESSENGER. Mariner 10 flew by me three times in 1974 and 1975. Only 45% of my surface was mapped. I am very temperamental, as you can see I still hold a lot of mystery.

Hi, I am Venus; do you know that I am the second planet from the sun?

Do you know that I am the sixth largest planet?

Do you know that I can be seen without using any special device?

Do you know that I am created to orbit in an almost circular pattern compared to any other planet?

This is not up for discussion my friends, I am the best!

Do you know that God made me one of the brightest objects in the sky after the Sun and the Moon?

Do you know that I Venus is only slightly smaller than the Earth? God created, blessed me and gave me all good things.

Do you know I move gracefully in a slow rotation?

Do you know that I do not have a magnetic field?

I am created to glorify God!!!!!!!!!!!!!!!!!

In the beginning, I Earth was without form, empty and in darkness until God called me to be!!!

Awesome!!!!!!

I the earth is the Lord's and all things in it.

I am the third planet from the Sun and the fifth largest:

I am divided into several layers which have distinct chemicals and properties

I spin around my axis every 24 hours,

Can you do that? She asked looking at the others

Wait, there's more; 71 Percent of my surface is covered with water.

My atmosphere is made up of 77% nitrogen, 21% oxygen, with traces of argon, carbon dioxide, and water.

I am unique because I am the only planet that has all the conditions needed for animals, plants, and humans to live in. I have plenty of water for them to drink.

I have air for plants and animals to use.

My temperature is just right to accommodate bacteria, protists, fungi, plants, and animals.

Obviously, you can see how favored I am!

I am the best!

People try to mess me up and pollute me, but my creator is teaching them to be kind to me.

I am the 4th planet from the sun

I'm wonderfully red

My surface is rocky and sandy

Scientists continue to investigate me hoping I can support life but that is not my job, so I will not be distracted.

My atmosphere has carbon dioxide so leave me alone!

I am RED to glorify God and that I will do all the days of my life.

The first spacecraft to visit me was Mariner 4 in 1965. Several others have followed.

I spin very quickly compared to other planets. I am happy to be me!

I told you, I am the best!

I am Mars

Hello, I am Jupiter!! Yes !!!!!!!

I am the largest planet in the solar system. I am made mostly of hydrogen, and I have 3 layers of clouds in me.

My first layer is made up of ammonia... I know you will say that STINKS but don't worry I am happy to be me. Just remember you use ammonia to clean your house!!!

My second layer is made up of ammonia and sulfur; while my third layer is made up of water vapor.

I have winds that blow as fast as 270 miles per hour.

Ok, more about me: I am so cool, God gave me BLINGS......ok.... Rings.........
Can any of you beat that?

God had pleasure in me and made me like this. I am the best!

Hello, I am Saturn, God made me so big I can be seen without a telescope.

I have lots and lots of hydrogen and helium. You need my gas to blow up your balloons!

However, my helium and hydrogen are in liquid form!!!! Isn't that cool? Can you beat that?

I am very big and have rings made up of rocks and ice.

I am a unique planet created to glorify my King.

I am the best.

Astronomers discovered me in 1781, but God created me before the beginning of time.

I am the 7th planet from the sun

One day on my planet is 17 hours long.

Also, I am the only planet that orbits on its side.

I am Uranus

I am the 6th planet from the sun

I am mostly made up of methane......a gas

My day is as long as Uranus too.....17 days

One year on me is 165 years on earth.

God made me unique such that the cloud pattern in my planet changes as I spin. Children would have a fun time playing with my cloud patterns if they were able to live on Neptune.

I am the brightest object in the night sky yet I have no light of my own!

I am the Earth's only natural satellite.

I am smaller than the Earth.

Man has visited me and even try to make me a god. I wish they will get wisdom and know that I have a creator.

On August 21, 2017, I moved between the sun and the earth; I caused total darkness for a period of 2 minutes and 39 seconds. It was amazing. The whole world stood to watch me move.

The animals thought it was night time! It is one of the most unforgettable moments of the century.

I moved like this 38 years ago, and I will be back soon.

I am the best. I am the Moon!

We are a system of stars, dust, and gas held together by gravity.

Our job is to shine and shine all day long and glorify God

Our galaxy is called the milky way.

We are too numerous to number.

Remember God promised Abraham in the beginning and I quote "I will surely bless you and make your descendants as numerous as the stars in the sky and as the sand on the seashore. God used us stars to express His plan for Moses;

So I am the best!

They kept discussing why they were the best until they got to the royal court where God had prepared a banquet. The King of Kings, their creator entered and sat on the throne. He was delighted to see all of his creation at the banquet.

They paraded themselves before God, and He asked them "what have you been up to?

They all looked at one another, then Saturn exclaimed, "Can you please put an end to this misunderstanding and let them know I am the best please?", then an argument ensued they all started talking about why they were the best repeating all they had said on the way to the galactic banquet.

God smiled and said

Dear Sun, the largest object in the solar system, you shine brightly for all to see.

Mercury, you have the most extreme temperature of them all, who can do what you do?

Venus, you orbit in the most circular pattern compared to other planets, unique.

Oh Earth, you spin on your axis every 24 hours and support life, how beautiful.

Mars, you spin much quicker than any other planet, displaying your red color with your rocky and sandy looking appearance.

Jupiter the largest planet in the solar system, full of special gases and winds that blow extremely fast.

Dear Saturn, you have rings made up of rocks and ice, your liquid hydrogen and helium flow continuously, you are a delight to behold.

Blue Uranus, you are the only planet that orbits on its side, and you make others realize how precious time, is.

Neptune, you contain mostly methane, a gas that can be used to produce electricity and heat buildings; how useful!

Moon, the brightest object in the night sky, you provide light for others, exceptional ability.

Stars, stars, stars, how beautifully shining every time, beautifying the galaxy".

They all shifted in their seats as they listened to him

God said "All of you are the best".

"Answer this question, can any of you perform the others job?"

"Sun, Mercury, Venus, Earth, Mars, Jupiter, Saturn, Uranus, Neptune Moon, stars, I ask again can you?"

They thought through the words that God said as each name was called. They paused, looked at one another and shook their heads.

"You are all unique, you all make me happy, you all have specific jobs that no other can do," God said

"You can do bigger things if you all work together instead of arguing over who is the best. You are all the best".

They finally realized there was no need for competition; they each serve a special purpose. They got together apologized to one another, gave a galactic hug and each bowed down to God their creator.

They danced and danced all night long. They never argued again.